STEVE ROGERS:
CAPTAIN AMERICA

» **_CAPTAIN AMERICA REMEMBERED_** finding out about the HYDRA organization and its leader, the evil Red Skull. He remembered a glowing cube—the Tesseract of Odin—and how Red Skull wanted to use its powers to take over the world. Cap defeated the Red Skull and the Tesseract was lost in the depths of the Atlantic Ocean. But the plane Cap was on had enough explosives to level half a continent, and he had to do something.

Captain America watched the arctic snow get closer and closer. This was not how he'd hoped it would all end. But it was better than the alternative. Captain America would go down with the plane, and the world would be safe. At least for now . . .

BILLIONAIRE INVENTOR TONY STARK was not having a good day. He wasn't even having a good week.

First, he was caught in an explosion in Afghanistan, where he suffered a near-fatal wound in his chest. To make things worse, the bomb that exploded had been made by Stark Industries—his own company. In fact, Tony had designed the bomb himself.

Too injured to escape, Tony was captured by enemy soldiers. They commanded him to build them a new weapon, the most powerful one he had ever created. If he did, they would let him live.

Tony got to work right away. And he did create the most powerful weapon he'd ever built. But it wasn't the one *they* expected. Or wanted. Instead, he built the weapon *he* wanted—the one he needed in order to escape.

Tony Stark built the Iron Man armor.

It was big and bulky and protected his heart. Bullets bounced off its surface without leaving a dent. The suit had its own weapons built in. And it could fly. Wearing the suit, Tony escaped.

When he returned home to California, he called a press conference to announce that Stark Industries wasn't going to build weapons anymore.

TONY STARK:
IRON MAN ≫

S.H.I.E.L.D DIRECTOR:
NICK FURY

TONY WANTED TO DEVOTE HIS TIME to designing a better version of the armor that had saved his life. He wanted to protect those in need, and he would do just that as the Invincible Iron Man.

Finally, people started to realize the truth. Tony Stark called for another press conference, and in front of reporters from around the world, he admitted he was indeed Iron Man.

After the press conference, Tony wanted to be left alone. Back at his mansion, Tony was greeted by J.A.R.V.I.S., the computer that ran both his enormous house and the Iron Man armor.

Then J.A.R.V.I.S. automatically shut down.

Tony was shocked. He had designed J.A.R.V.I.S. himself . . . and Tony's designs never failed.

"'I am Iron Man,'" a voice said from the darkness, echoing Tony's earlier words. "You think you're the only Super Hero in the world? Mr. Stark, you've become part of a bigger universe. You just don't know it yet."

"And exactly who are you?" Tony asked as the figure moved closer.

"Nick Fury, director of S.H.I.E.L.D." A tall, muscular man stepped out of the shadows. He wore a patch over his left eye. "I'm here to talk to you about the Avenger Initiative."

WHEN IT CAME TO GAMMA RADIATION, there was no one who knew more than Dr. Bruce Banner.

So it wasn't surprising that the military came to Bruce in search of a permanent cure for gamma-ray poisoning. But what he didn't realize was that General Ross and the military actually wanted something else: they were trying to re-create the long-lost Super-Soldier Serum that had created Captain America.

If Bruce had known, maybe he wouldn't have volunteered to be the first test subject for his own experiment.

It didn't work.

Bruce Banner began to struggle against the straps holding him down. And suddenly they ripped apart like wet paper. Because Bruce Banner was gone. Where he had been, there was now a giant green goliath.

THE INCREDIBLE HULK.

Eight-and-a-half feet tall and bursting with muscle, the Hulk was fueled by anger and emotion.

The Hulk ripped the room apart, throwing heavy equipment as though it were made of cardboard. He hurled himself at the wall and went crashing through the concrete and steel as if it wasn't even there.

THE HULK HAD ESCAPED.

BRUCE BANNER:
THE HULK »

S.H.I.E.L.D. DIRECTOR NICK FURY wanted Tony Stark to join a team of individuals who were similar, in some ways, to Iron Man. Tony, naturally, was of the opinion that no one else was anything like Iron Man.

Tony was sitting in the center of a giant plastic doughnut on the roof of a bakery, thinking about Nick Fury's proposal, when Fury tracked him down.

"Sir," said Fury, "I'm going to have to ask you to exit the doughnut."

"I told you, I don't want to join your supersecret boy band," Tony said.

Fury laughed. "No, no, no, I remember—you do everything yourself. How's that working out for you?"

NATASHA ROMANOFF:
BLACK WIDOW >>

» **INSIDE THE DOUGHNUT SHOP,** Tony looked around. "Where's the staff here?"

A beautiful woman strode up to the table, but she wasn't a waitress. "We've secured the perimeter," she said to Nick Fury, "but I don't think we can hold it too much longer."

Tony was stunned, which was rare. The woman who had approached them was clearly a S.H.I.E.L.D. agent. What shocked Tony was that he knew her. She was Natalie Rushman—one of his paralegals.

"Huh," Tony said to her. "You're fired."

"That's not up to you," she said calmly, sitting down.

"Tony," said Fury, "I want you to meet *Agent* Natasha Romanoff."

"I'm a S.H.I.E.L.D. shadow," Natalie—or, rather, Natasha—explained. "I was tasked to you by Director Fury."

"What do you want from me?" Tony asked.

"What do we want from you?" Fury repeated. "What do you want from me? Contrary to your belief, Mr. Stark, you are not the center of my universe. I've got bigger problems."

Bigger problems than Tony Stark? Tony found that very hard to believe. What could possibly be bigger than him?

"YOU GOT ANY IDEA WHAT THIS THING IS EXACTLY?"

said the man with the flare as he motioned to the squalls of snow whipping up and over the arctic's many snow-dunes.

"It's probably a weather balloon," replied one of the men from Washington.

"I don't think so." Their guide chuckled. He led them to the discovery.

"What is this?" asked the man from Washington, looking at what appeared to be some sort of giant aircraft.

The men used a laser to cut a hole in the top of the aircraft and lowered themselves on ropes into the pitch black interior. Their flashlights moved back and forth in the darkness.

Something caught the eye of the man from Washington. It was . . . what? A star, circles . . . under a layer of frost. It seemed to be red, white and blue.

"Give me a line to the colonel," said the man from Washington.

"It's three a.m. for him, sir."

"I don't care what time it is," the agent replied. "This one's waited long enough."

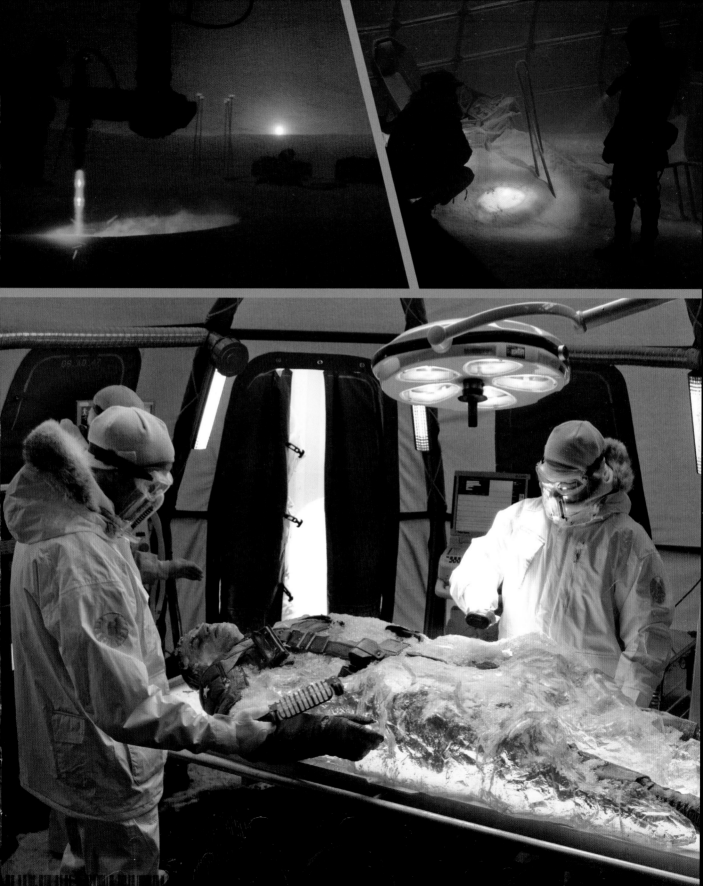

STEVE ROGERS OPENED HIS EYES. He sat up and looked around the room. It was a bright, pleasant space, with a soft breeze blowing through an open window. There was a baseball game on the radio. It seemed like a perfect day.

"Good morning," a nurse said as she walked in. "Or should I say afternoon?"

"Where am I?" Steve asked slowly.

"You're in a recovery room in New York City." The nurse smiled.

Steve didn't smile back. "Where am I really?"

"I'm afraid I don't understand," the nurse said, still smiling.

"The game," Steve replied, tilting his head toward the radio. "It's from May 1941. I know because I was there. Now I'm going to ask you again—where am I?"

Suddenly, armed guards entered the room. Steve bashed his way through a wall and started to run.

He found himself outside, in an area that looked vaguely like New York City's famous Times Square.

» EXCEPT...IT WASN'T THE TIMES SQUARE

Steve remembered. Everything was all wrong: the stores, the cars, the way people dressed . . .

"At ease, soldier," a voice said.

Steve paused. Captain America wasn't impressed easily, but there was something in the man's voice that got his attention.

An imposing man in a long trench coat stepped forward. He wore a patch over his left eye. Steve didn't know it, but he was talking to Nick Fury, and Fury knew he would need America's Super-Soldier to rejoin the fight.

"I'm sorry about that little show back there," Fury said, "but we thought it best to break it to you slowly."

"Break what?" Steve asked.

A look of regret and sympathy passed quickly over the man's face. "You've been asleep, Cap. Frozen for almost seventy years."

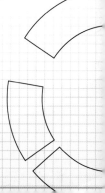

>> ***THERE IS A REALM*** that exists alongside our universe. It is not a planet: no astronomer can see it; no astronaut can visit. It is one of the Nine Realms that are ruled by gods and goddesses for whom magic and science are one and the same.

IT IS CALLED ASGARD.

This mystical Realm is ruled by Odin Allfather, a wise and just king. He has kept Asgard safe—and usually at peace.

Odin has two sons: Thor and Loki. Both are smart, strong, determined and brave. But they have always been opposites in many ways.

Thor, heir to the throne of Asgard, was good-hearted, even if his pride and his anger often got the best of him. Loki, second in line, seemed calm and nice. But deep down, he was jealous and angry and greedy.

Loki was determined to change things, no matter what the cost. Either he would become the ruler of Asgard . . . or Asgard would be destroyed. So Loki set a trap for Thor, who almost caused a war between the Realms.

Thor was saved by Odin, but rather than being thankful, Thor lashed out, yelling at his father and calling him weak.

To teach Thor humility, Odin stripped him of his powers and his mighty war hammer, Mjolnir, and sent him to Earth to live as a mortal until he overcame his pride.

THE MIGHTY
THOR »»

DURING HIS BRIEF TIME ON EARTH, Thor learned empathy and the joy that comes from helping others. And once he learned humility, Thor was immediately restored to his full power. With mighty Mjolnir in his grip again, Thor returned to Asgard just in time to stop Loki from stealing the throne.

Loki was determined to take over Asgard, to punish Odin and Thor, who he now saw as his greatest foes, despite the love he had always felt for them.

It was not to be. Thor triumphed in the end.

But sly Loki was not so easily defeated. After seeming to be lost to the void of space, Loki appeared on Earth and located the greatest power in the universe—the Tesseract.

Loki knew just how he wanted to use it.

NICK FURY WAS NOT A HAPPY MAN. His organization, the Strategic Homeland Intervention, Enforcement, and Logistics Division—or, as everyone called it, S.H.I.E.L.D.—was experiencing some . . . difficulties.

Fury looked around at S.H.I.E.L.D. agents Phil Coulson and Maria Hill. They were two of the people he trusted with his life. But after what happened with agent Clint Barton, could he trust anyone?

Clint Barton was one of S.H.I.E.L.D.'s best agents. Clint was codenamed Hawkeye, and for good reason: he had insanely accurate aim—especially with the bow and arrow, his favorite weapon. Bright, tough, and loyal, Barton had recently been compromised by a being not of this world, and now all of Earth was at risk.

Hawkeye had been assigned to guard scientist Dr. Erik Selvig, who was studying the Tesseract at a secret S.H.I.E.L.D. bunker. Nick Fury and S.H.I.E.L.D. wanted to know exactly what the Tesseract was and what it could do. They had some idea—but they needed more information.

>> DR. ERIK
SELVIG

CLINT BARTON:
HAWKEYE >>

» *SO THEY TURNED TO DR. SELVIG.* Selvig was a leading researcher in his field and had also come in contact with Thor during the Norse god's brief stay on earth.

But Selvig had not only come in contact with Thor—he'd also come in contact with Thor's evil brother, Loki.

And it was through Dr. Selvig that Loki learned the location of the Tesseract. Using all his powers, Loki appeared on Earth and brainwashed both Dr. Selvig and Hawkeye.

Despite Agent Hill's and Director Fury's valiant efforts to stop them, Loki escaped with not only the Tesseract, but with Hawkeye and Dr. Selvig.

Director Fury now had an even better idea of just how important and powerful the Tesseract was—and just how important, powerful, and dangerous Loki was.

Nick Fury knew he had to step up his game. And he knew who to turn to for help.

BUT IT WASN'T GOING TO BE EASY.

BRUCE BANNER WAS ON THE MOVE. He knew S.H.I.E.L.D. was after him. And he knew General Ross wanted to capture him—to experiment on him more.

Bruce wasn't going to let that happen. General Ross thought he understood how dangerous the Hulk was. But he didn't. Ross thought they knew how powerful the Hulk could be. But he didn't. Bruce knew that only he truly understood what the Hulk could be—for good and bad.

So he worked on keeping the Hulk under control. In the past, whenever Bruce had gotten angry or scared, the Hulk had come out. But Bruce was learning how to control his emotions—and the Hulk. He was also learning how to get upset without turning into the Hulk.

Bruce was trying to protect himself and the world from the Hulk. But for now, he had to stay away from S.H.I.E.L.D. until he had learned how to totally control *THE HULK.*

BUT NO ONE COULD HIDE FROM S.H.I.E.L.D. FOR LONG.

They found Bruce in Calcutta, working as a doctor, trying to help the poorest of the poor. He was with a patient one day. When he looked away for a moment, the patient had disappeared. In her place was a beautiful S.H.I.E.L.D. agent. She said her name was Natasha Romanoff.

"How did you find me?" Bruce asked sadly.

"We never lost you," she replied. "I'm here, alone, on behalf of S.H.I.E.L.D. We need you to come in."

Natasha said that they weren't looking for the Hulk—they needed Bruce Banner. Something called the Tesseract had been stolen, she explained, possibly by a being once worshipped as a god. S.H.I.E.L.D. needed to find it before the thief could use its power, but it was emitting gamma radiation at levels too subtle for any of their tools to trace. Bruce was the world's leading expert on gamma radiation, and they needed his expert advice right now.

Bruce suddenly yelled, "Stop lying to me!"

Natasha—known within S.H.I.E.L.D. as Black Widow—was not surprised often. But now she jumped and braced herself to face the Hulk.

Then Bruce began to laugh.

"I'm sorry," he said teasingly. "That was mean."

STEVE ROGERS TRIED TO GET USED TO HIS NEW WORLD.

But it wasn't easy. Everything was so different. No one used pay phones in phone booths anymore—now everyone had little pocket-size phones they carried around with them everywhere.

There was only one place he still felt comfortable: the gym.

Steve was working out when Nick Fury walked in.

"Are you here with a mission, sir?" Steve asked.

"I am."

Steve nodded. "Trying to get me back in the world?"

Nick Fury paused. "Trying to save it," he replied.

Fury explained that the Tesseract—the object Steve had seen Red Skull using in his attempt to destroy the world—had been stolen. Steve knew how powerful the Tesseract was—and how dangerous it could be in the wrong hands.

Nick Fury didn't ask Steve if he would help. "I've left a debriefing packet at your apartment," he said simply. Then he left.

Captain America looked up. He might not understand this brave new world. But the importance of saving it . . . that was something he understood.

TONY STARK WAS IN HIS APARTMENT at the new Stark Tower skyscraper in New York City when a video monitor suddenly lit up.

"I need to speak with you," said S.H.I.E.L.D. agent Phil Coulson.

Tony had met Agent Coulson before—but Tony didn't want to have anything to do with S.H.I.E.L.D. now.

Then Tony's private elevator opened and Agent Coulson stepped into Stark's apartment. "I need you to look at this," he said, handing Tony a briefcase.

Despite his reservations about the Avengers Initiative, Tony was curious.

Agent Coulson explained that the threat S.H.I.E.L.D. was facing now was so great that they would need all the help they could get.

Tony opened up the briefcase. Inside were holographic images containing information on Captain America, Hulk, Thor—and Iron Man himself.

But what really got Tony's attention was the Tesseract. Tony had an idea of what it was . . . and what it could do. He knew that if it fell into the wrong hands it could spell disaster. And in the hands of something greater than human, there was no telling where—or if—the devastation would end.

TONY STARK WAS IN.

AGENT PHIL COULSON WAS STARSTRUCK. As part of his duties for S.H.I.E.L.D. he had met a Norse god and he had defied Iron Man. But he couldn't believe he was actually sitting with his idol.

He escorted Captain America aboard the S.H.I.E.L.D. aircraft carrier. There they met Bruce Banner and Black Widow. Bruce was also thrilled to meet one of his heroes. Black Widow acted the way she usually did—like she didn't care about anything or anyone.

The aircraft carrier began to move. To the surprise of many, however, it didn't head for open water. Instead, it rose into the air. Tony tried not to show his surprise, but inside, a thousand questions ran through his brain at once—wondering how they were powering it, who'd designed it, who'd built it, and more.

"THANK YOU ALL FOR COMING," Nick Fury said, appearing on deck.

He turned to Bruce—of everyone there, Bruce looked the most uncomfortable.

"As soon as the Tesseract is back in S.H.I.E.L.D.'s hands," Fury assured him, "you can go. I'm not going to keep you here."

Bruce smiled politely, clearly not believing a word of it.

"The Tesseract is emitting gamma radiation, and no one knows about that better than you," Fury explained.

Agent Coulson informed Bruce that S.H.I.E.L.D. had access to any device connected to a satellite. At Fury's directive, S.H.I.E.L.D. agents set Bruce up in a lab with spectrometers and an endless supply of devices that could be used to track the Tesseract.

It didn't take long for Bruce to track the Tesseract's unique energy.

>> **THOR'S LITTLE BROTHER, LOKI,** was on the run in Germany. But the master of mischief couldn't resist using his newfound powers to make the people of Midgard bend to his will. So when he saw a crowd gathered outside a museum in Stuttgart, Loki decided to have some fun. He approached a guard and commanded him to kneel. To the guard's shock and horror, he found himself falling to his knees.

"All of you," Loki shouted. "Kneel!"

Everyone dropped to their knees . . . except for one man. Somehow, he had remained standing. "I do not kneel to men like you," he said.

"There are no men like me," Loki replied.

"There are always men like you," said the old man.

Loki lifted his staff and pointed it at the man. He fired a bolt of energy.

There was a whoosh, a blur, and a loud clang. Something had come out of nowhere and deflected Loki's energy bolt before it reached the old man, then circled back around, almost faster than the eye could see.

» *IT WAS CAPTAIN AMERICA'S SHIELD!* The Super-Soldier caught the returning shield with ease. It had been a very, very long time since he had last used it—but it felt to him like it had been only yesterday.

"Ah, the Super-Soldier from the Great War," Loki sneered.

"It wasn't that 'great,'" Captain America replied.

"Mine will be." Loki grinned as the two began to fight.

ABOVE, NATASHA WAS PILOTING S.H.I.E.L.D.'S QUINJET. She had hoped to stun Loki with a blast, but there were too many innocent people around for her to get a clean shot.

Her radio filled with static. No, it wasn't static—it was heavy metal music.

"Hello, Tony," she said with a smirk.

Iron Man zoomed past the Quinjet and swooped down to the square. He fired repulsor blasts at Loki, but they weren't as effective as he'd expected.

So Iron Man used his repulsor ray to blast Loki's staff out of the villain's hands.

FACED WITH THE COMBINED MIGHT of both Captain America and Iron Man, Loki threw up his hands in defeat. He was surrendering . . . but the evil smile on his face made both heroes very uneasy. They did not trust the villain.

Back in the Quinjet, Black Widow, Iron Man, and Captain America stood guard over Loki. Nick Fury radioed in, telling them to get Loki to the S.H.I.E.L.D. Helicarrier. They'd continue the search for Hawkeye, Selvig, and the Tesseract later. The main thing was to make sure it wasn't in Loki's hands—and that he was kept somewhere he could do no more harm.

Natasha, piloting the Quinjet, noticed dark black clouds rolling over the jet. She looked around. The rest of the sky was crystal clear.

"Where's this coming from?" she said, as the clouds began to ripple with lightning. Low, rolling thunder rattled the jet.

Loki looked more nervous than anyone.

"What's the matter?" Captain America asked. "You scared of lightning?"

"I'm not overly fond of what follows," Loki replied.

There was a huge crack of thunder, and they felt something massive land on top of the jet.

Captain America and Iron Man got ready to face whatever was out there. Natasha checked one of the jet's cameras. She saw a man in battle armor. She recognized him from S.H.I.E.L.D.'s files. It was Thor.

» **IRON MAN** ordered the gangway of the Quinjet to be lowered so he could fly out.

"Wait!" Captain America warned. "He might be friendly!"

"Doesn't matter," Iron Man responded. "If he's come to rescue our prisoner . . ."

As the ramp began to descend, a pair of hands suddenly grabbed it and ripped it all the way open.

Before Iron Man could fire a repulsor blast, Thor flung Mjolnir. The hammer sent Iron Man tumbling across the Quinjet. Out of control, he bashed into Captain America. With both Iron Man and Captain America down, Thor was able to grab his brother. He caught Mjolnir, and a moment later Thor and Loki were gone.

Iron Man and Captain America looked at each other in disbelief. Then, moving faster than Captain America could believe, Iron Man rocketed out of the ship after them.

Captain America grabbed a parachute.

"Are you crazy?" shouted Natasha. They were thousands of feet up, the Quinjet was moving at a supersonic clip, and—as far as she knew—Captain America couldn't fly. "Maybe you should sit this one out," she suggested.

CAPTAIN AMERICA SIMPLY SALUTED HER. . . AND JUMPED.

THOR AND LOKI HAD LANDED ON A MOUNTAIN.

"We thought you were dead," Thor said to his brother. "We mourned. Our father . . . "

"Your father!" Loki replied. "Did he not tell you my true parentage?"

"Loki," said Thor, "we were raised together. Played together. Fought together. Do you remember none of this?"

"What I remember is growing up in your shadow," Loki said bitterly.

Thor looked at his little brother, the brother he couldn't help but love, despite everything Loki had done. "You must return to Asgard. We will talk to the Allfather. . . . "

"I am not going anywhere," Loki said. "If Asgard can't be mine, then I shall rule over Midgard."

Thor's patience ran out. "You know nothing of ruling," he shouted.

Something suddenly plowed into Thor: the invincible Iron Man. Although taken by surprise, Thor quickly fought back, and the two heroes fiercely battled one another.

THOR BEAT IRON MAN WITH MJOLNIR, rocking him with blow after blow. But each time Iron Man regained his footing, Thor would knock him back down. And with every blow, it became more and more difficult for Iron Man to pick himself back up.

Thor raised Mjolnir and summoned all of the power available to him. A great column of lightning descended from the skies and poured into Tony's armor.

But inside the Iron Man suit, J.A.R.V.I.S. alerted Tony to something unexpected: the lightning had fed the suit with an unprecedented power surge. Rather than destroying the armor, his power was now at 400-percent. Iron Man didn't waste the chance—he blasted the Norse god with a repulsor blast so powerful it knocked down even the mighty Thor.

Somehow, Thor did the impossible: he got back up. As Thor and Iron Man faced off again, something red, white, and blue shot down between them.

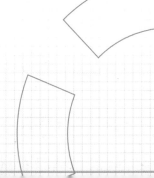

» **CAPTAIN AMERICA** stood with his shield raised. His body language made it clear: it was time for the fighting to stop.

Instead, Thor swung Mjolnir over his head. He brought it down with all his might.

Captain America raised his shield to meet the hammer. Mjolnir slammed into the vibranium, and a sonic boom shook the entire mountain. But Captain America didn't budge.

The three heroes stared at each other, then over toward Loki. The god of mischief, the reason they were fighting, merely smirked.

Thor grabbed his brother and brought him back to the Quinjet. Thor would force Loki to cooperate with S.H.I.E.L.D. for now. After what Thor had learned about his brother's desire to conquer Earth, it seemed the right thing to do.

LATER

>> ### *BACK ON THE S.H.I.E.L.D. HELICARRIER,* Bruce Banner watched as Loki was locked up in a huge glass cage.

"This wasn't meant for me, you know," Loki taunted Bruce. "It was constructed for someone angrier and greener."

Loki's words struck home. Bruce felt his heart rate increase. He breathed deeply to calm down.

Agent Coulson radioed in. With Loki captured, his control over Hawkeye and Selvig had faded. Barton had the Tesseract and was on his way back to S.H.I.E.L.D.'s carrier with it and Dr. Selvig.

Loki was trapped and the world was safe—at least for now. Thor waited aboard the Helicarrier, ready to return his brother to Asgard to face Odin's strong arm of justice.

Steve, Natasha, Tony, and Bruce looked at one another and then over at Thor. None of them could have captured Loki alone. It was only together—despite their rocky start—that they were able to prevent what could have been the end of the world.

And if the problem was even too big for all of them to face, Fury knew he could call upon Dr. Banner to transform into the incredible Hulk to lend a large, green hand.

Nick Fury was right: *THE WORLD NEEDED THE AVENGERS.*

And even though they would now go their separate ways, whenever a threat was too much for one hero to handle, S.H.I.E.L.D. could call upon Captain America, Iron Man, Hulk, Thor, Black Widow, and Hawkeye—and the Avengers would assemble!